TRACTOR MAC

CERTIFICATE OF REGISTRATION

· · ·

This book belongs to

_____

ALSO BY BILLY STEERS

TRACTOR MAC
TUNE-UP

Written and illustrated by
BILLY STEERS

FARRAR STRAUS GIROUX · NEW YORK

Dr. Lou stopped by that afternoon.
"I've never felt like this before,"
Mac told his friend Sibley the horse.

"Hmmm," said Dr. Lou as he listened to Tractor Mac and checked his engine. "This is serious, Farmer Bill. It could be worn bearings or a bent connecting rod. You should bring Tractor Mac to my shop tomorrow."

"I don't want to go to the hospital," groaned Tractor Mac to his friends that evening. "What if I can't be fixed? What if they sell me for parts? Why does this have to happen to me?"

"Don't worry, Tractor Mac. You'll be okay," mooed Margot the cow.

"We want to see you get better," clucked Carla the chicken.

"I'll give you my lucky horseshoe," said Sibley.

"You can have my four-leaf clover for good luck," said Sam the ram.

The next day, Farmer Bill brought
Tractor Mac to Dr. Lou's Tractor Clinic.
"You'll be back to work soon,"
said Farmer Bill.

Tractors lined the yard of the clinic. There were types of tractors Mac had never seen before.

"Bring him right in," Dr. Lou said to Farmer Bill.

"You've got nothing to worry about," wheezed a giant tractor on steel wheels.

"Gus is always right," said a little riding mower.
"My name is Gasket. We've been here a long time . . .
But you're a *work* tractor! You get to be fixed up first."

Tractor Mac was wheeled into a clean workroom.

Dr. Lou and his helper, Steve, checked their tools and went straight to work.

Mac's oil was drained, his hood removed,

and the valve cover and cylinder head lifted off.

Then the pistons and
rings were checked
and repaired.

The sleeves and connecting rods were examined, and the engine block, oil pump, and crankshaft inspected.

Replace, repair, rebuild, and re-grease!
Tractor Mac was then given a full tune-up
with new spark plugs and wires.

"You sound much better now!"
cheered Gasket.
"It's back to work for you!" puffed Gus.
Tractor Mac smiled. "I do
feel much better, thanks."

"He'll make a full recovery," said Dr. Lou, beaming. "What a good patient he was."

Farmer Bill was happy to hear Mac's smooth *chugga, chugga, chugga* again.

RECOVERY AREA

TIRES

Tractor Mac was soon back at work.
"That's a healthy tractor!" clucked Carla.
"A real trooper," said Sam.

"I love the sound of a well-tuned tractor," mooed Margot.

Late that summer, Tractor Mac saw Gus and Gasket at a farm show.

"Dr. Lou fixed you," said Mac. "You're just like new!"

"I'm better than new!" exclaimed Gasket.

"I'm fit as a fiddle in my work clothes!" said Gus.

"Hooray for tractor fixers!" cheered Tractor Mac.

When Giants Roamed the Earth
Make: International
Year: 1909

To the Tenczas and all tractor fixers, young and

old, who make tired iron run like new again

Farrar Straus Giroux Books for Young Readers
175 Fifth Avenue, New York 10010

Color separations by Bright Arts (H.K.) Ltd.
Printed in China by Toppan Leefung Printing Ltd.,
Dongguan City, Guangdong Province
Designed by Kristie Radwilowicz
Previous edition published by Tractor Mac, LLC
First Farrar Straus Giroux edition, 2015
1 3 5 7 9 10 8 6 4 2

mackids.com

Library of Congress Cataloging-in-Publication Data
Steers, Billy, author, illustrator.
  Tractor Mac tune-up / Billy Steers. — First Farrar Straus Giroux edition.
    pages cm
  Originally published in Roxbury, Connecticut, by Tractor Mac in 2011.
  Summary: "Tractor Mac is scared that he has to take a trip to Dr. Lou at the tractor hospital,
but with the help of his animal friends and some other machines who have stopped in for
a tune-up, he learns that going to the doctor doesn't have to be scary at all" —Provided by
publisher.
  ISBN 978-0-374-30108-8 (paper over board)
  [1. Tractors—Fiction.   2. Hospitals—Fiction.   3. Medical care—Fiction.]   I. Title.

PZ7.S81536Tv 2015
[E]—dc23
                                                                          2014040399

Farrar Straus Giroux Books for Young Readers may be purchased for business or promotional
use. For information on bulk purchases please contact Macmillan Corporate and Premium
Sales Department at (800) 221-7945 x5442 or by email at specialmarkets@macmillan.com.

ABOUT THE AUTHOR

Billy Steers is an author, illustrator, and commercial pilot. In addition to the Tractor Mac series, he has worked on forty other children's books. Mr. Steers had horses and sheep on the farm where he grew up in Connecticut. Married with three sons, he still lives in Connecticut. Learn more about the Tractor Mac books at www.tractormac.com.